THE Kissing CONTEST

Other Apple Paperbacks
you will enjoy:

That's What Friends Are For
by Carol Adorjan

After the Fortune Cookies
by Mary Blakeslee

Glass Slippers Give You Blisters
by Mary Jane Auch

Boys Are Yucko!
by Anna Grossnickle Hines

Eat Your Heart Out, Victoria Chubb
by Joyce Hunt

THE *Kissing* CONTEST

Dian Curtis Regan

AN
APPLE
PAPERBACK

SCHOLASTIC INC.
New York Toronto London Auckland Sydney

ISBN 0-590-43911-1

Copyright © 1990 by Dian Curtis Regan.
All rights reserved. Published by Scholastic Inc.
APPLE PAPERBACKS is a registered trademark
of Scholastic Inc.

12 11 10 9 8 7 6 5 4 3 2 1   0 1 2 3 4 5/9

Printed in the U.S.A.   40

First Scholastic printing, December 1990

For Carlene, Kathy, Linda, Donna,
Jan, Cathy, Claudia, and Joanne.
Then and now, the best.

THE Kissing CONTEST

1

Kelsey Minor wrote her name in the upper right-hand corner of the test paper in the fancy new style she'd been practicing all week.

She dotted the *i* in Minor with a little heart and swirled four of the letters to underline her whole name. It looked like this:

Kelsey Minor

Under that she wrote *Fifth-Grade Spelling Test.*

Then she stared at the back of David Bonicelli's head.

"Number one." Mr. Hale's skinny six-foot frame rose from behind his desk and leaned against the chalkboard. "Airplane."

As Mr. Hale used the spelling word in a sample sentence, Kelsey made up her own sample sentence inside her head: *David Bonicelli and I flew our airplane into the Oklahoma sunset.*

"Number two." Mr. Hale moved away from the chalkboard. The back of his green vest was blotched white with chalk, looking as if someone had thrown a giant powder puff at him. A few kids snickered.

Kelsey concentrated on writing *airplane* in her fancy new style, dotting the *i* with a tiny heart.

"Code," said Mr. Hale. "Number two is code."

"David Bonicelli and I talk in a secret code known only to us," Kelsey whispered to herself in place of Mr. Hale's sample sentence.

"Number three. Rescue."

I rescue David Bonicelli as he hangs by his fingertips above the shark-infested pool.

Mr. Hale began his traditional spelling test walk around the edge of the classroom. He always started his walk between the third and fourth spelling words, and completed his circling of the desks on word number twenty.

Kelsey glanced at her best friend, Andrea Giese. Andrea pretended to yawn. Kelsey covered her own mouth with one hand to keep from laughing out loud.

Just once, they wished Mr. Hale would do something different.

Like walk in the other direction.

Begin his circle on the second word.

Or the fifth.

Walk up the center aisle.

Trip.

Anything different!

Mr. Hale was as predictable as a pencil sharpener.

Kelsey accidentally wrote *rescue* in her old unfancy style. She rubbed her pink eraser over the word and wrote it the fancy way, ending the *e* with a little curlicue.

"Wedding," Mr. Hale said, continuing his slow circle. "Word number four is wedding."

Kelsey smiled to herself as she thought up all kinds of possibilities for her next sample sentence.

2

"What are you going to be for Halloween?" Andrea asked as they waited for the bus after school.

"I don't know," Kelsey answered.

Andrea flipped her red hair over the top of her head and hung it upside down, giving her head five violent shakes. Then she shook her mane over her shoulders, letting the tousled ends tumble down her back in disarray. Andrea never combed her hair. She liked the wild look.

"What are *you* going to be for Halloween?" Kelsey asked, brushing back her own dark hair, which was too short and straight to be wild.

"A rock star." Andrea gave her head another shake for good measure.

"Why? Because they all have messed-up hair?"

"No." Andrea tsked-sighed. "Because I like to sing."

"Oh." Kelsey tried to think of something she liked to do that she could be for Halloween. She liked to swim. That's why she kept her hair short. She thought about coming to school wearing nothing but her swimsuit. *Bad idea.*

The school bus arrived, whining and groaning as it ground to a stop. Kelsey wondered why school buses always sounded as if they were in great pain.

"Well, you'd better decide fast," Andrea said, boarding the bus ahead of her, "because Halloween is next Friday."

Kelsey slid into the seat next to Andrea. "I'll think about it over the weekend."

All the kids on the bus were chattering about what they were going to be for Halloween.

"A dancer."

"A monster."

"An alien."

"A game show host." That one got a lot of laughs.

Andrea leaned close to whisper into Kelsey's ear. "Are you going to sit next to *him* at the party?" Her wild hair fell across Kelsey's notebook.

"Sit next to who? At what party?"

Andrea gave another tsk-sigh. "Sit next to David Bonicelli at our class Halloween party."

"Shhhhhhh!" Kelsey's eyes darted to the kids around her to see if anyone had overheard Andrea's words.

"I'm whispering," Andrea whispered.

"You whisper too loud."

"Well?

"Well, what?"

"Are you going to kiss — ?"

"What!?"

"I mean *sit*."

"You said *kiss*."

"My tongue slipped." Andrea burst into giggles.

Kelsey pretended to be in shock — because she *was* in shock.

"Really," Andrea said, gulping air between giggles. "I *meant* to say, are you going to *sit* next to him?"

Kelsey waited until Andrea stopped gulping, then whispered, "I don't know if I have enough nerve to sit next to him." She gave in to the giggles, too. "And I could never kiss him in a zillion years. Not even if we had a kissing *contest!*"

Instantly two heads appeared over the top of the seats in front of them.

"Did you say kissing contest?" asked one of the heads: Brina Kenton.

"What a fantastic idea!" said the other head: Molly Day.

Kelsey's temperature shot up five hundred degrees. They'd heard her!

Andrea's giggles turned into hysteria.

"When is the kissing contest?" came a voice from behind them.

"At the Halloween party next Friday," answered Brina.

"Fantastic!" exclaimed Molly. Molly liked to say *fantastic*. It was her favorite word.

Kelsey slumped in her seat and willed herself to disappear.

"Who's putting on a kissing contest?" came two voices from across the aisle.

"Kelsey Minor," answered Brina and Molly.

Andrea's hysterics slid her off the seat and onto the floor of the bus.

Kelsey grabbed the shoulder of Andrea's jacket and pulled her back into her seat. "Look what you started."

"Me? I didn't say anything about your contest."

"*My* contest?" Kelsey hissed. "*What* contest?"

Andrea grinned and shook her wild hair. "The *kissing contest* you're putting on next Friday at our class Halloween party!"

3

Kelsey spent the entire weekend trying to decide what she was going to be for Halloween. Each idea seemed too normal: a witch, a princess, a hobo.

Her mom suggested a ghost, but no one dressed like a ghost anymore. She wanted to be something unique.

Kelsey rode her bike to Andrea's house on Sunday afternoon. She watched Andrea try on every single piece of clothing in her closet until she pulled together a rock star outfit that was outrageous, yet believable. Still, it didn't give Kelsey any ideas about a costume of her own. Ah, well, she had a few more days to make up her mind.

On Monday morning, Kelsey missed the bus. Her mom drove her to school before going on to the university where she took classes.

Kelsey stepped from her mother's car, waved good-bye, then trotted across the schoolyard. The nippy autumn wind ruffled her hair and spiraled colorful leaves away from her feet as she ran.

The instant she joined the fifth-grade line in the spot Andrea had saved for her, the usual loud jabbering shut off like a water sprinkler.

Everyone's eyes were glued to her.

"What's going on?" Kelsey whispered.

"You!" Andrea shot back.

"Me?"

"You and your kissing contest."

Andrea had a funny look on her face, making Kelsey suspect her best friend had helped the contest rumor spread through the fifth grade faster than David Bonicelli downhilled on his killer skateboard.

"Yeah, Kel," called Brina. "Tell us the rules for the contest."

"Can anyone compete?" asked Molly.

"Kissing!" shouted Adam Alldredge. "Yuck!"

Girls on both sides of Adam slapped at him.

Kelsey had laughed off the episode on the bus going home last Friday because kids were always a little crazy before the weekend. She never dreamed Andrea's slip of the tongue would grow into such a big deal.

"Are you going to be the judge?" came a voice from behind her.

It was David Bonicelli! He was talking to her!

"Me? Judge?" Kelsey heard her voice squeak.

She hated it when her voice squeaked.

"Yeah," the others chimed in. "Who's gonna pick the winner?"

Andrea held up one hand as if she were the referee. "It's Kelsey Minor's contest," she stated, sounding a little like Mr. Hale. "And Kelsey will decide who, what, when, where, and how." Now she *really* sounded like Mr. Hale.

The bell rang. Lines snaked toward the building.

Kelsey grabbed Andrea's arm and pulled her from the line. She waited until everyone had passed. "Andrea, what are you doing?"

"Nothing."

"Why didn't you tell everyone there's no such thing as a kissing contest?"

"Because there *could* be."

"What do you mean? There *could* be."

"We have contests for perfect attendance, spelling contests, contests for the most books read, the highest high jump jumped, the lowest note sung in music — I won that one, remember? And contests to see who can finish the multiplication drills the fastest."

Andrea stopped to take a breath. "See? We have contests for everything, so why not a contest for kissing?"

Kelsey was fascinated in spite of herself. "But what does that have to do with *me?*"

"You're the one who came up with the idea, so

you get to plan it, and, you know, set the rules. It's the idea of the year."

"Girls!"

They both jumped as Ms. McFarland, the gym teacher, yelled at them, "You'll be late. Let's go!"

Andrea started off toward the school building. Kelsey walked backwards in front of her, trying to slow her down. Her friend always seemed to know what was going on when Kelsey didn't. Maybe Andrea could tell her what to do.

"But . . ." Kelsey paused, putting both hands on top of her head to emphasize her confusion. "I don't know what a kissing contest *is*."

Andrea took hold of Kelsey's shoulders and spun her frontwards. "You will," she said, giving her a friendly shove. "By Friday."

4

"*G*ood *morning fifth-graders*," Kelsey mumbled to herself.

"Good morning fifth-graders," exclaimed Mr. Hale with his every-morning-at-nine-o'clock enthusiasm. He pulled out his attendance roster.

"*If you're absent today, please raise your hand.*"

"If you're absent today, please raise your hand."

"*Chuckle, chuckle*," Kelsey said to herself. It had been funny the first day of school, but now it was October. Were they doomed to hearing the same jokes every day for the entire year?

After the usual morning rituals, Kelsey tried to concentrate on her reading assignment. It was about kids in Norway getting a holiday from school this week to harvest potatoes.

At least they *used* to harvest potatoes — in the old days. Now they got a short vacation from school to do other things. The holiday was called *Potetserie* — Potato Days.

But every time Kelsey got to the second page of the story, something made her glance up.

Kids were smiling at her.

Kids who *never* smiled at her.

Like Mellisa Tucker.

Or David Bonicelli.

Mellisa had even sharpened a pencil for her, and David had picked up her jacket this morning after Adam Alldredge knocked it off its hook.

Why was everyone so nice to her all of a sudden?

Is this what being popular was like?

All because of a contest that didn't exist?

Kelsey turned the page in her reading book and stared at a picture of nineteenth-century Norwegian kids digging potatoes under a huge Scandinavian sun and dropping them into brown burlap bags.

Part of her felt like standing at her desk, right then and there, and shouting, "Look, guys, there *is* no kissing contest, there never *has* been a kissing contest, and there never will *be* a kissing contest."

And another part of her said, "If this is what being popular is like, I think I'm going to enjoy it while it lasts."

A shadow fell across the page of her reading text. Kelsey looked up.

Mellisa, Brina, and Molly huddled over her left

shoulder. "Will you eat lunch with us today?" Brina whispered.

Kelsey stared at them, wondering if they'd mistaken her for somebody else.

Somebody popular.

She raised her shoulders in a shrug.

"Fantastic!" Molly gushed.

Kelsey returned her attention to the reading assignment, starting over again on page one of the potato story. But it was no use. Potatoes were the last thing on her mind.

In order to keep this instant popularity going, she'd have to come up with a *real* contest.

Slumping at her desk, she closed her reading book as well as her eyes. *I'm creative*, she said to herself. *Maybe if I concentrate hard enough, I can invent some kind of competition that — with any luck at all — might vaguely resemble whatever a kissing contest is supposed to be. . . .*

5

"**M**om," Kelsey began, carefully loading plates into the dishwasher after dinner. "Have you ever competed in a contest?"

"What kind of contest?" her mom asked, looking up from the pile of accounting textbooks scattered in front of her on the kitchen table. She seemed grateful for the question so she could stop studying for a few minutes.

"*Any* kind of contest."

"Let me see." Mrs. Minor tapped the keys on her calculator as she thought. "Well, in high school, I was on the swim team. That was very competitive."

"What were some of the rules you had to follow?"

Kelsey's mom grinned at her. "Are you thinking about joining the swim team when you get into high school?"

"Ummm." Kelsey dried her hands with a towel,

then reached for her notebook and pencil, stalling. This is not the way she'd meant for the conversation to go.

"Sure," she said, biting the end of her pencil. "I might join the swim team. But right now I'm more interested in rules."

"Well, okay." Her mom imitated Kelsey, biting the end of her pen. "The rules I remember were:

"Don't start until the whistle blows."

Kelsey jotted it in her notebook.

"Don't hold your breath."

She wrote that down, too.

"And, oh yes, this was the coach's favorite — give it all you've got."

Kelsey's pencil scribbled across the page.

"Thanks, Mom," she said, heading for the hallway.

"Kel, wait."

She stopped to listen.

"Have you decided what you're going to be for Halloween?"

Kelsey shook her head.

"Please think about it, dear. It'll probably take a couple of days to get a costume together."

"I know."

"Remember last year?"

Kelsey laughed. "We stayed up half the night trying to make me look like an alien from outer space."

"Yeah, by one o'clock in the morning, we *both* looked like aliens from outer space." Her mom opened her accounting book. "Promise you'll make up your mind soon?"

"Promise."

Kelsey rounded a corner and found her dad reading in the family room. Groucho, her black-and-white cat, sprawled across his lap, looked as though he were reading the book along with her dad.

She opened the notebook, tapping her pencil point on the page to get her father's attention. "Have you ever competed in a contest?"

He looked up from his book. "Sure I have. Lots of times. The last one was my triathlon."

"What were the rules?"

He laid down his book and took off his glasses, smiling. "What a surprise, Kel. Are you training to be in a triathlon?"

"Da-ad." He always interpreted things she said the wrong way. She could probably handle the swimming part, but not the running and cycling, too. "I just want to know the rules."

Looking disappointed, he ruffled Groucho's fur. "Well, some of the rules I remember were:

"Train hard for the event.

"Eat spaghetti the night before.

"Keep drinking water.

"And, whatever you do, don't stop until you're finished."

Kelsey copied his words into her notebook.

"Why spaghetti?" she asked.

"Because your body has more energy if you load up on carbohydrates before an endurance event."

"Oh." Dads were always so logical. She kissed him on the cheek. "Thanks."

"Is that all you wanted?"

"That's all." Kelsey reached to pet Groucho, tickling in between his back toes the way he liked.

"What kind of contest are you planning?"

"Contest?" *There he goes again, reading between the lines.*

"Well, I assumed from your questions, you're organizing some kind of competition at school."

"Sort of." *Feeble answer, Kelsey.*

"So, what will you be doing in this contest?"

"Um." She backed toward the doorway, hoping to avoid further questions. "We'll be, um . . . digging potatoes."

Kelsey couldn't believe those words had come out of her very own mouth, but how could she tell her dad she was organizing a kissing contest?

She somehow wished it *were* a potato-digging contest. It sounded a lot less complicated. Except for the fact they'd have to *grow* the potatoes before they could dig for them.

Both her father and Groucho gave her puzzled looks, then went back to their book.

Kelsey groaned all the way down the hallway to her room. What were her chances of convincing the entire fifth grade that a potato-digging contest would be much more challenging and fun than a kissing contest?

6

Tuesday was even worse than Monday. News of the kissing contest had now spread throughout the entire school.

Kids who didn't know who Kelsey Minor was the week before, knew now. Not only knew, but stopped and stared at her as she walked down the hall, or when she was at recess or lunch.

For the second day in a row, it was hard for her to concentrate on her reading assignment. The October holiday in the morning's story was *Rainmaking Day* in South Africa: *The queen of the Lovedu people puts secret medicine into her rain pot, then the children dance until rain begins to fall.*

Kelsey thought about the dance they'd had last year when she was in fourth grade. At first, the teachers said no. But the class begged and begged until the teachers finally gave in.

Everyone in class brought music tapes from home.

20

Then nobody danced.

Nobody.

It was so embarrassing.

If it were up to the fourth-graders of Oklahoma to dance for rain, the state would be as parched as a sandbox.

A note fluttered onto the page of Kelsey's reading book.

She glanced up to see if Mr. Hale was watching. He was at his desk, putting in his contact lenses.

That meant it was lunchtime. Mr. Hale always took off his glasses and put in his contact lenses right before the lunch bell rang.

Every single day.

Kelsey unfolded the note, smoothing it on top of her book:

Dear Kelsey,

Did you bring your lunch today? If so, let's eat at our special place.

Your friend, Andrea G.

Kelsey's heart skittered. Brina, Molly, and Mellisa had asked her to eat lunch with them again today.

She'd already said yes.

Andrea hadn't minded eating alone yesterday. But two days in a row? Maybe she should invite Andrea along, too. Would the others mind?

Sometimes her friend acted a little weird. It

21

was okay around Kelsey because they'd been friends forever, but what would the others think?

The lunch bell rang.

Andrea caught up with her at the door. "So, you want to go outside?"

Their special place to eat was on the brick wall that linked the school to the chain fence. Kids who brought their lunch could eat either in the cafeteria or outside.

"Um, I'm staying in today," Kelsey answered, trying not to look into Andrea's eyes.

"Why?"

"I think it's going to rain."

Andrea tsked-sighed.

"Come eat with me in the cafeteria." Kelsey knew her invitation sounded insincere.

"Are you eating with *them?*" Andrea rolled her eyes and pushed the tip of her nose up with one finger.

Kelsey shrugged. "Maybe. So what?"

"All they do is comb their hair and talk about boys."

Kelsey had noticed, too, but it hadn't really bothered her. Except she had nothing to add to the conversation — even when they asked her who she liked.

Kelsey figured they'd think she was a baby if she said "No one," so she'd told them, "It's a secret."

She'd die if they knew she liked David Bonicelli.

Kelsey waited for Andrea to quit making faces. She desperately needed to talk to Andrea because she needed advice on planning the kissing contest. After all, Andrea was the one who'd gotten her into this whole mess in the first place.

"I'd *rather* eat lunch with you," Kelsey said.

"Then, let's go." Andrea walked across the classroom and opened the outside door.

The sun was shining.

There was no sign of rain.

Kelsey followed, unsure what to do. "Well, I already told the others I'd eat with them."

Andrea flipped her wild hair and went out the door, letting it slam in Kelsey's face.

Feeling a mixture of exasperation and relief, Kelsey hurried to the cafeteria and joined the lunch line.

Mellisa, Brina, and Molly waved to her from their table and pointed to an empty chair they'd saved.

Just for her.

It made Kelsey feel special.

Well, half of her felt special.

Her other half was trying not to think about the hurt look that had clouded Andrea's face right before she'd slammed the door.

7

When Kelsey got up Wednesday morning, rain was falling. She wondered if the queen of the Lovedu people had anything to do with it.

Since the gloomy weather matched her mood, Kelsey dressed in gray cords and a gray sweatshirt.

The week was half over and she still didn't know what she was going to be for Halloween.

Or what she was going to do when Brina announced in the middle of the Halloween party that it was time for the kissing contest to begin.

And Kelsey knew, as sure as Mr. Hale got his hair cut every other Tuesday after school, that Brina would do it.

She had a lot of thinking to do and only two days to do it.

On the bus, Andrea sat in the last row by herself and stared out the window at the gusting rain.

Molly told Kelsey she could squeeze in with her and Brina, so she did.

Then the bus driver, Miss Matthews, hollered at Kelsey that three on a seat was against the rules.

Kelsey had to sit next to Adam Alldredge because nobody else would. He burped the Oklahoma song all the way to school until Kelsey plugged her ears with her fingers.

Mr. Hale greeted her at the classroom door. He was wearing blue slacks, a blue-checkered shirt, and a blue tie. Every single Wednesday, Mr. Hale wore the same clothes.

The fifth-graders called Wednesdays *Blue Day*.

"Miss Minor," he began, stopping her by pressing one finger into the top of her shoulder. "I hear you have a surprise for the class Halloween party."

Kelsey gasped. Had someone told the teacher about her kissing contest? Were they crazy?

She thought Mr. Hale looked a little worried when she nodded. What should she say? How much did he know?

"Well, we'll leave plenty of time for your, um, contest, is it?"

Kelsey nodded again. "Okay, sir. Thank you."

Why couldn't he have said, *"I'm sorry, Miss Minor, but we won't have time for your contest on Friday. Maybe some other time. Like when you're in the twelfth grade."*

She glanced around the room. Brina and Molly were huddled in one corner, giggling.

Kelsey joined them, now that they were almost her best friends. "What's so funny?" she asked.

"Andrea Giese," Molly snickered. "Just look at her."

The sound of Molly snickering at Andrea made Kelsey heat up with anger.

Her eyes darted to her best friend's desk. Andrea was wearing her Gummi Bear pajama top as a shirt over pink sweatpants with flip-flops for shoes. On top of that, she wore her vampire cape from last year's Halloween costume.

Andrea's bangs were spiked straight up in the air. The rest of her hair was caught in one bushy ponytail over her left ear — on which she had drawn three squiggly stars with red ink. And, she was wearing purple-framed glasses. Andrea never wore glasses. What was she doing?

Kelsey glanced around the room. All the kids were making fun of Andrea, who had her nose in a book, ignoring everyone. It embarrassed Kelsey as much as if *she* were the one sitting there in her pajama top and all the other weird things Andrea was wearing.

There was nothing Kelsey could do but take her seat. A sudden urge to protect her friend washed over her. Ripping a piece of paper from her notebook, she fished a pencil out of her desk to write Andrea a note:

Dear Andrea,

Kelsey paused. For the first time in her life, she had nothing to say to her best friend.

Hi!!! she scribbled in her fancy hand-writing.

Then, *your friend, Kelsey*

Folding the paper, she walked to the pencil sharpener, dropping the note onto Andrea's desk as she passed.

While Kelsey sharpened her pencil, her eyes stayed on Andrea, who read the note, but didn't write back.

Andrea *always* wrote back.

When Kelsey returned to her desk, there were three notes addressed to her, stacked in a pile.

She opened the one on top. It said:

> CAN'T WAIT
>
> *Mellisa*

The second note said:

UNTIL

Brina

The third note said:

LUNCH !!!!!!!!!!!!!!!!!!!!!!!!!!!

Molly

Cute. Kelsey groaned to herself. She knew why they couldn't wait until lunch.

They couldn't wait until lunch because she and her big mouth had promised to announce a list of rules for the nonexistent kissing contest.

8

"Little Hito hurried through the streets of Tokyo, carrying a *bettara* given to him by a street vendor. It was a large pickle, dangling from a rope, and was part of Japan's October holiday to honor Ebisu, one of the Seven Gods of Luck."

Kids began to giggle at Mr. Hale's dramatic reading. Kelsey could hear Molly snickering all the way in the back row.

After the story was finished, Kelsey tried to answer her workbook questions about the pickle-on-a-rope tradition, but her eyes kept darting to the clock.

Lunchtime was getting closer and closer. The fifth grade was about to discover the horrible truth about her.

She didn't know the rules for the kissing contest any more than little Hito did.

When Mr. Hale cleared off his desk to insert his contact lenses, Kelsey's heart began to thump.

She knew the minute his contacts were in place, the lunch bell would ring. With Mr. Hale around, they didn't need a clock in the room.

Kelsey took her time putting away her reading book. Maybe Andrea would invite her to eat outside again. Then she could tell the others she couldn't sit with them today. They'd have to wait until later to find out the contest rules.

Later, after she'd made them up.

When the lunch bell rang, Andrea flew outside without even looking at her. Kelsey's heart twinged with regret.

Now she'd have to face the *terrible trio*. But maybe that would be less painful than walking across the playground next to her best friend while everyone pointed and laughed.

"Come on, come on, come on," urged Molly, pulling Kelsey from her desk. "We have to get seats together today so we can all hear your rules."

Kelsey trudged down the hallway after her three new friends, wondering why being popular left such a troubled knot in the pit of her stomach.

Today's lunch was burgers and chips with a green dill pickle on the side. Fifth-graders got into trouble because half the class was playing with the pickles, pretending they were *bettaras*, dangling from ropes. Ms. McFarland, who was on lunch duty this week, had no idea what was going on.

Mellisa munched on a potato chip, opening a notebook she'd brought into the cafeteria.

Brina lent Mellisa a pencil, then all three of them leaned toward Kelsey.

"We're ready," Brina said.

Kelsey choked on her burger.

"Come on, come on, come on."

Molly was starting to get on her nerves.

What should she do? Confess right here and now that there weren't any rules for the kissing contest? And the reason there weren't any rules was because there wasn't any contest?

On the other hand, Kelsey liked the way the three most popular girls in class had been paying attention to her all week. Maybe she could stall them and save face.

The interview with her mom and dad flashed through her mind. But she'd brilliantly left the list of rules she'd gotten from her parents back in the classroom. Could she remember them all?

"Quit stalling," Brina ordered.

"Okay, I'm ready." Kelsey closed her eyes to think, trying to picture the page from her notebook in her mind. When she opened her eyes, a half dozen more kids had joined their table.

"Rule number one," Kelsey began.

The small crowd seemed to hold its breath, waiting for her to continue.

"Don't start until the whistle blows."

Mellisa jotted down the first rule while Molly

repeated it slowly, "D-o-n-'t s-t-a-r-t u-n-t-i-l t-h-e w-h-i-s-t-l-e b-l-o-w-s."

"Hush, Molly," Brina scolded. "Let Kelsey talk."

"Number two," Kelsey continued. "Don't hold your breath."

All mumbled their agreement.

"Three." Kelsey was beginning to feel like Mr. Hale giving the Friday spelling test. "Give it all you've got."

Embarrassed laughter tittered through the ever-growing group around the table.

"Four. Train hard for the event."

"Fantastic," whispered Molly.

"Five. Eat spaghetti the night before."

"Wha-a-a-t?" Adam Alldredge made his presence known.

"Shush," said Brina. "She knows what she's talking about."

Kelsey had never received so much attention in her whole life.

Except for the time in second grade when she got sick all over Mrs. Shipp's desk after eating too much Valentine candy.

More kids joined the table. Kelsey's palms began to sweat from speaking before such a large audience.

She avoided looking to her left, because that's where David Bonicelli leaned against the table on his elbows. If she looked at him, she knew she'd heat up until she melted into a puddle.

A Kelsey puddle.

"Is that all?" Molly asked.

"No, there's more." Kelsey squinted at the ceiling, trying to remember the rest of the rules.

"Number six. Keep drinking water."

Adam snickered.

"And number seven. Whatever you do, don't stop until you're finished."

It was so quiet, everyone could hear Mellisa's pencil scribbling across the page.

"Fantastic," Molly whispered again, looking over Mellisa's shoulder. "Can I copy the rules from you?"

"Me, too," came scattered voices from around the table.

"What's going on here?" Ms. McFarland leaned over the mass of fifth-grade bodies, trying to see what was holding their attention. "Let's hustle outside." She clapped her hands a few times as everyone grabbed at Mellisa's precious list.

Mellisa sat on her notebook to keep snatching hands away from it. "My father has a copy machine," she told them. "Tomorrow, I'll bring enough copies for everyone."

Kelsey was forgotten as the group rushed toward the playground door, huddled around Mellisa and her list of useless rules, as if she were a queen bee.

After taking one bite of the pickle, Kelsey

dumped her barely eaten lunch and went outside. She spotted Andrea alone, hanging upside down from the top of the monkey bars. Her vampire cape tickled the ground in the chilly fall breeze.

Andrea could hang upside down longer than anyone. She said it was good for her hair. Kelsey had tried it, but it always killed the backs of her knees after two seconds.

The afternoon bell rang. Still, Kelsey headed toward Andrea, weaving her way through kids rushing to line up.

After all, Andrea was her best friend, and they'd barely talked the last three days. This week's traumas would be much easier to bear if she could share them all with Andrea.

Molly caught Kelsey by the sleeve, flipping her around. "I'm so glad you're not friends with Andrea Giese anymore," she said in a loud voice. "That girl is *weird*."

Kelsey let herself be pulled along with the crowd, back toward the school building.

She sighed, mentally pinching herself for being disloyal to her best friend.

Wait until tomorrow, Kelsey told herself. Andrea will be back to normal. You can make up with her then.

9

After lunch, Kelsey got permission to go to the library. She set her notebook on a table by the back window where she could have some privacy.

Running her finger along a set of encyclopedias, she pulled out the *K* volume and carried it to the table. She checked to her left and right to make sure no one was watching. Then she flipped through the pages, searching for the word *kiss*.

She would die if anyone peeked over her shoulder and caught her looking up *kiss* in the encyclopedia.

It wasn't there.

Terrific. How was she supposed to find ideas for her kissing contest if *kiss* wasn't even in the encyclopedia?

Kelsey let the book fall shut with a loud smack, glancing up to see if the librarian had heard. He was busy helping a third-grader reach a high shelf.

She moved to the computer, hunting for the *k*

on the keyboard. There it was. *K*, she typed. Right above it was the *i*. Then it took her half a minute to find the *s*. She hit it twice.

The computer churned for a few seconds, then flashed NO ENTRY.

"What are you doing?" came a voice from behind her.

Kelsey jumped. It was David Bonicelli.

"Nothing." Her fingers turned into long ice cubes, refusing to fly across the keys, typing anything that would wipe the word *kiss* off the screen.

Kelsey hunched her shoulders over the computer, trying to block David's view. She picked out the letters to the word *Japan* so he'd think she was doing her reading homework.

He moved to the computer next to her.

Now what was she going to do? She'd planned on typing different versions of *kiss* until the computer took the bait and gave her the information she needed.

But she couldn't stand there with David Bonicelli peering over her shoulder, and type words like *smack*, *peck*, or *smooch*. He'd think she was a pervert.

What else could kissing be called? An art? A sport? A custom?

Custom sounded good. Kelsey deleted the word *Japan*, then picked out the letters *c-u-s-t-o-m*. Remembering how to spell the word was difficult with David standing so near.

She watched him out of the corner of her eye, wondering if he were watching her out of the corner of his.

The computer made more churning noises, then flashed a long list of books on social customs.

Ah ha. Kelsey felt pleased. It was a start. And it looked as if she were actually working on a real school project. She copied the information, then blanked the screen.

Kelsey wished she could keep standing next to David Bonicelli for the rest of the school year, but she had important work to do. She gathered her things, then moved to the nonfiction shelf.

Choosing several books, she returned to her table and spent the rest of library time reading more than she ever wanted to know about the custom of kissing, copying bits and pieces of information into her notebook.

As she looked through the texts, one of the references caught her eye. *Kissing Games* it said, *page 139*. Feeling excited, Kelsey flipped to the right page. The book explained the rules to games called spin the bottle, post office, flashlight, and secret draw.

Kelsey felt herself blushing as she read the rules. Mr. Hale would die if she announced games like these at their Halloween party.

She would die first — of embarrassment. A kissing *game* was not the same thing as a kissing *contest*.

Kelsey kept turning pages. Secretly, she hoped to find an obscure listing buried deep in the middle of one of the reference books that said, *Kissing Contest: In ancient times, young people competed in a contest for kissing. And the rules were . . .*

Then all she'd have to do was borrow someone else's competition. Unfortunately, no one in the course of history had ever invented such a thing.

It was all up to her.

Kelsey opened another book on customs, and stared at a picture of the man who invented cornflakes, John Kellogg. She pretended she was looking at her own picture in the book as a world-famous inventor.

The idea of *going down in history* intrigued her. But is that what she wanted to be famous for? Inventing a kissing contest? Would it humiliate her parents?

"We'd like you to meet our daughter, Pastor. She's in all the history books, but we can't tell you what she invented."

The recess bell interrupted Kelsey's daydream. Gathering her things, she returned to class, wishing John Kellogg had taken time to invent a kissing contest right after he invented cornflakes.

10

"**K**elsey, I've called you three times and you haven't answered me."

Kelsey felt a whoosh of air as a pillow was lifted off her head. She opened her eyes, focusing them on her mom's worried frown.

"Are you feeling all right?" Mrs. Minor asked, cupping one palm across Kelsey's forehead.

"Yes. I mean, no. I mean, yes."

Kelsey knew better than to fake being sick. Each time she tried, it backfired. She'd end up getting sick for real a few days later when there was something special she wanted to do.

Her mom opened the window curtains. Sunlight flooded the room, depressing Kelsey. In the back of her mind, she'd hoped there'd be a raging blizzard outside, canceling school for the rest of the week.

The month.

The year.

"Get up or you'll be late for the bus."

Kelsey groaned. Today was Thursday, which meant tomorrow was Friday. She had only one more day before the fifth grade discovered she was a fraud.

By tomorrow, her reputation would be in smithereens.

She'd be an outcast forever.

Maybe she could borrow a jar of pickles from the refrigerator and some rope from the garage, then move to Tokyo and make her living selling *bettaras* on street corners.

"What are you going to be for Halloween?" Kelsey's mom said, asking the now-dreaded question from the doorway.

"I don't know."

"Kel-sey, tomorrow is the big day. When are you planning to get your Halloween costume together? In December?"

Kelsey pulled herself from under the bedcovers. "I don't know." Her bare feet smacked the floor as if to punctuate her words.

Her mom sighed. "We go through this every year," she said to the ceiling as she closed the door.

Kelsey was so slow showering and dressing, she didn't have time to sit down for breakfast. When her mother wasn't looking, she snitched a handful of Halloween candy her dad had set out early. It should keep her from starving to death before lunchtime.

Kelsey dumped the handful of chocolate candy into her bookbag, then grabbed more for her pocket.

When the school bus arrived at the corner, she climbed on board. Brina and Molly were sitting together as usual, and Mellisa was sitting with her third-grade cousin. The only kids sitting by themselves were Adam Alldredge and Andrea.

"Make up your mind," Miss Matthews said, tapping Kelsey's shoulder. "I can't take off until you're seated."

Adam grinned at her and burped, "Hello, Kelsey Minor."

Kelsey stepped past him to the back of the bus, sliding into the seat next to Andrea. "Hi," she began, then gasped as Andrea faced her.

Andrea had drawn a rainbow on her left cheek. Each stripe was a different color of ink. Surrounding it were tiny stars. On Andrea's right cheek in green ink were her initials: A.U.G. Andrea Ursula Giese.

Today she wore her pajama bottoms, which were really sweatpants, decorated with the tiny Gummi Bears. On top was a Batman T-shirt, which matched her Batman tennis shoes. On each wrist was every bracelet Andrea owned, including three Kelsey had given her.

Andrea gazed at her as if she were a stranger. She didn't return Kelsey's hello.

"Why?" was all Kelsey could think to ask.

41

"Why what?"

"Why are you wearing your pajama bottoms to school?"

"Shush!" Andrea's wild hair, worn loose today, whipped one way, then the other as she looked to see if kids were watching them.

They were, but not because of anything Kelsey had said.

"These aren't pajama bottoms."

"Yes, they are. You had the top on yesterday. And you wore them to bed when I spent the night with you two weeks ago."

Andrea reached to arrange her bangs, still spiked toward heaven. All the bracelets on her wrists jingled together. "These are *not* pajamas. It's a jogging set," she explained. "Sometimes I wear it to bed."

Kelsey was trying to ignore the disapproving looks coming her way from Mellisa, Brina, and Molly. She hoped all three of them got cricks in their necks from craning to get a good look at her.

Her conversation with Andrea was going nowhere. "I don't *care* if they're pajamas or not, just tell me why you're doing this."

"Doing what?"

"Dressing weird."

Andrea looked down at her clothes as if she didn't know what Kelsey was talking about.

"And yesterday, too. Why did you wear your vampire cape to school?"

"For Halloween."

"Halloween isn't until tomorrow."

"I like to celebrate all week long." Andrea flipped her eyelashes up and down and jingled her bracelets. "I call it *Halloweek*."

Kelsey groaned. Maybe she should change the subject. "Do you want me to eat lunch with you outside today?" She knew once they got to school and the other kids saw what Andrea was wearing, it'd be all over for her friend.

The fifth grade might forgive Andrea's weirdness for one day, but not for a whole week.

A Halloweek.

"Why do you want to eat lunch with me?"

Kelsey had asked herself the same question. Andrea was her best friend in the whole world, and — after the Halloween party tomorrow — Kelsey planned to be real short on friends, best or otherwise.

In spite of Andrea's peculiar ways, Kelsey still felt loyal. "You're my best friend," she said, as if that explained everything.

"Ha!" Andrea blurted, a bit too loudly, drawing more stares.

The school bus ground to a stop. Andrea climbed over Kelsey before she could move out of the way, then pointed a bony finger at her the same way Batman was pointing at her from the front of Andrea's T-shirt. "You've got three too many best friends." With that, Andrea sprinted down the aisle, hurrying to be first off the bus.

By the time the bell rang, and all the fifth-graders were settled in, everyone was buzzing about two things — Andrea, who was now called *Aug* because of the green ink initials on her cheek — and the rules for tomorrow's kissing contest.

Mellisa had made enough copies of Kelsey's list so no one in class had to share the rules.

And she'd run the copies on bright pink paper, the same color as Pepto-Bismol.

Kelsey slumped to her desk. Everywhere she looked, kids had their eyeballs glued to the pink papers.

Molly flitted around the room, passing out the last of them. She flipped one onto Kelsey's desk, then snatched it up again before Kelsey could move to touch it.

"Whoops," Molly gushed. "I guess you don't need a list because you're the one who made up these *fantastic* rules."

Kelsey buried her head in her folded arms. Her stomach was in such turmoil right now, not even a giant dose of real Pepto-Bismol could save her.

11

Kelsey scrunched the stack of notes on top of her desk into a ball. Trudging to the wastepaper basket, she threw them away. When she returned to her desk, four more notes were piled there:

Dear Kelsey,

I have a question about the rules for the kissing contest. How can I keep drinking water if I'm not supposed to stop until I'm finished?

Brina

Dear Kelsey,

I hate spaghetti. Do I really have to eat it tonight?

Molly

Dear Kelsey,

Want to borrow my whistle for tomorrow's contest?

Molly (again) ☺

Dear Kelsey,

I told my dad about your list of rules for the kissing contest. He's calling Mr. Hale this morning.

Adam Alldredge

Kelsey sighed. In the old days — B.C. — before the contest, she loved getting notes, but no one had ever sent them to her except Andrea. Today they were plopping onto her desk like raindrops from a spring cloudburst.

What was wrong with Mr. Hale? Why didn't he catch kids passing notes to her? Why didn't he suspend her from school for a few days? That would solve a problem or two.

Kelsey twisted in her desk to see what Mr. Hale was doing. He was leaning against the water fountain in the back of the room, not paying attention to her or anyone else. His attention was riveted on the Pepto-Bismol paper clenched in his hands.

Molly had given the teacher a list of the kissing-contest rules!

"Terrific," Kelsey mumbled.

Shoving the notes into her desk, she grabbed her reading book and opened to today's story. At times like this, it was best to act like a model student.

Kelsey waited for Mr. Hale to press his finger into the top of her shoulder. But he didn't.

He seemed unusually quiet today, calling reading groups as he normally did.

Yet, every time Kelsey looked at him, he was watching her. Mr. Hale was probably waiting for her to do something weird.

Maybe he suspected a little of Andrea's weirdness had rubbed off on her, since the two had been best friends forever.

Kelsey moved a chair to her reading group, thankful for a break from the raining notes. Today's October holiday story was about a celebration in India called Pushkar Fair. The Hindus believed their creator had formed a huge lake at Pushkar by dropping a lotus petal from above.

This month, thousands of pilgrims gathered by the lake to celebrate. The highlight of the fair was the Camel Rush. Competitors ran as fast as they could, then jumped onto a sturdy camel to see how many people would fit without falling off.

As Mellisa read the story out loud, Kelsey watched Mr. Hale — when he wasn't watching her. He didn't act surprised at the strange Camel Rush tradition at all.

So how could Mr. Hale think she was weird by staging a kissing contest? Weird was jumping onto a camel to see how many people it would hold.

12

Kelsey jumped off the bus and dashed down the street to her house. Maybe if she got away fast enough, no one else would ask her about the kissing contest. Kids were starting to sound like her grandmother's parakeet, asking the same questions over and over.

Only they weren't saying, "Do you want a treat?" "Do you want a treat?" They were saying things like, "What time is the kissing contest?", "Who gets to go first?", and "What is the winner's prize?"

Kelsey arrived out of breath at her house, unlocked the front door, then slipped inside. Her mother had a late class on Thursday afternoons, so Kelsey always beat her home.

Dumping her books onto the desk in her room, Kelsey shut the door, kicked off her shoes, and flopped onto her bed next to Groucho. She buried herself under a quilt to block out the questions still tumbling through her mind.

Only now the questions were, "How did you get yourself into such a terrible mess, Kelsey Minor?", "Do you know how unpopular you'll be tomorrow after everyone finds out you made this whole thing up?", and "Why have you deserted your best friend for new friends you don't even like?"

As Kelsey grew sleepy, the questions faded from her mind. But they were replaced with new questions — bits and pieces of what she'd learned at the library yesterday: "How did the custom of kissing begin?", "Why does the groom kiss the bride at the end of the wedding ceremony?", "Why do movie stars pretend to kiss in greeting, but don't?"

Kelsey snuggled further under the quilt. The only thing she'd accomplished all week was to learn more facts about kissing than anyone else in the fifth grade.

Now she was a kissing expert.

A kissing expert who'd never been kissed.

She chuckled to herself.

Then her chuckle turned into a groan. All the kissing trivia in the world wasn't going to save her tomorrow.

Suddenly Kelsey's eyes shot open. She bolted upright, flinging the quilt aside. Groucho yowled and sprang away.

"That's it!" she cried, hopping from the bed and fumbling through her notebook. "One, two, three, four," she counted out loud. "Four pages of trivia about kissing!"

Kelsey danced around the room in her stocking feet, holding the notebook above her head like a trophy. The fifth-graders loved trivia — *any* kind of trivia. Tomorrow, she would give them a kissing contest after all. A kissing *trivia* contest!

Sorting through her desk drawers, she found a package of lined notecards. For the next two hours, Kelsey made up kissing questions, penning them neatly on each card in her fancy handwriting. *Why did Prince Charming kiss Sleeping Beauty?*

Kelsey paused, holding her pencil in midair. Was that question too easy?

Nope, she said to herself. She needed a few easy questions for kids like Adam Alldredge. He could never remember which cupboard held the math workbooks, and which cupboard held the hamster food.

Under the question she wrote: *To wake Sleeping Beauty from a hundred-year sleep.*

Nibbling on Halloween candy, Kelsey chose another card. *How can you sign a love letter with a kiss?*

Answer: *Sign it with an* X.

Pleased, she popped a Hershey's Kiss into her mouth. Ah, ha! She grabbed another card, writing, *What is printed on the streamer coming from the top of a Hershey's Kiss?*

Answer: *Hershey's Kisses.*

"What are you doing?" came her mom's voice from the hallway.

The door opened. "Homework?" Mrs. Minor asked, looking pleased to catch her daughter working without having to be told.

"Sort of," Kelsey answered, shoving her math book on top of the cards before her mom could read any of them.

"Time to eat," Kelsey's mother said. "Then after dinner, we'll have to whip you up some kind of a Halloween costume for tomorrow." Her mom gave her the same look she did whenever Kelsey asked her to bake brownies for school treats late on the night before they were needed. "You *have* decided what you're going to be for Halloween, haven't you?"

"Sure," Kelsey lied as her mom disappeared down the hall. She'd been so caught up with trivia questions for the kissing contest, she'd forgotten all about putting a costume together.

Kelsey gathered the notecards and placed them in her bookbag for tomorrow. Then she scrunched leftover foil from the Hershey's Kisses into a silver ball, tossing it into the trash can.

"*Hershey's Kisses,*" she whispered to herself, suddenly connecting the name of the candy to what she'd been nibbling.

It gave her a wonderful idea.

Kelsey reached into her pocket and pulled out

another piece of the silver teardrop candy.

She sat it on her notebook, hunching over to study it.

"Kelsey, you're a genius," she whispered to herself. "Not only will I show up tomorrow at the Halloween party with a genuine kissing *contest*, I'll also show up as a genuine *kiss*!"

"Kel! Come to dinner!" her dad called.

"Coming!" Quickly she scribbled a new trivia question onto a notecard. *What did the inventor of the kissing contest go to the Halloween party as?*

Answer: *A Hershey's Kiss.*

13

Kelsey and her parents were up half the night assembling her Halloween costume.

Searching the corner of the basement where her dad stored leftover boxes from Christmas, Kelsey chose the biggest one. She cut a huge circle out of the bottom of the box. Then she cut two holes for her legs.

Kelsey's mom helped her unravel and straighten a pile of coat hangers, then punch one end of them through the cardboard. They fashioned a teardrop frame with the hangers, leaving an opening fastened with a hook at the top so Kelsey could get into the costume.

Kelsey found a few rolls of heavy aluminum foil stashed away with the barbecue supplies, while her mom bent two more wire hangers around the bottom of the cardboard to anchor the foil. Kelsey's dad volunteered to help so they could all get to bed at a decent hour.

The long part of the project was fastening thin

material around the teardrop frame before covering it with silver foil. They almost forgot to leave armholes.

While her parents smoothed foil over the frame, Kelsey ironed one of her white ribbons to use as the streamer from the top of the kiss.

In blue marker, she lettered the words *Hershey's Kisses* over and over until she ran out of ribbon.

The last thing Kelsey did before going to bed was to dig out her gray tights so her legs would somewhat match the silver foil. Then she put her costume into a huge lawn-and-leaf bag so she could carry it on the bus without kids seeing what it was. She wanted it to be a surprise when everyone changed into their costumes during lunch.

"Get to bed," Kelsey's mom said when they finished.

Kelsey was happy to obey.

"And next year," her mom added, "decide what you're going to be for Halloween in August because *that's* when we're making your costume."

Kelsey woke with a start, feeling as if she'd taken a roller-coaster ride instead of sleeping. Troubled dreams had tossed and turned her through the night, forcing Groucho to sleep on top of her desk instead of cuddled by her side.

Why was she troubled?

Today was Halloween.

She had a costume to wear. A costume she really liked.

And she'd finally invented a *real* kissing contest.

She wasn't going to let the fifth grade down after all. She'd still be popular. And she'd win back her best friend.

So why did she feel so scared?

Because you're tricking them, Kelsey. The entire fifth grade is hoping to be kissed today.

Expecting to be kissed today.

By somebody.

ANYBODY.

Except Adam Alldredge, her mind argued back. *He didn't want to kiss anyone and no one wanted to kiss him.*

But, Kelsey, no one gets kissed at all during your so-called kissing contest.

Everyone is probably using gallons of mouthwash this morning.

Just in case.

Kelsey sat up in bed to plead with Groucho. "But I did the best I could."

Groucho didn't seem to care enough to open his eyes and look at her.

"I mean, the whole idea of *kissing* during a kissing contest is ridiculous, Groucho, because no one in the fifth grade even knows how to kiss.

"Except maybe Mellisa," she added, remembering last year's rumor that Mellisa had kissed a sixth-grade boy from the middle school by the bicycle rack.

But that doesn't count, Kelsey. They're still going to be disappointed.

And angry with you for deceiving them.

"But, Groucho, if we actually kissed, who would *win* the kissing contest? The fastest kisser? The funniest kisser? The best kisser?"

Groucho answered with a flick of his white-speckled tail.

"And how am I supposed to *judge* the contest if we really kiss? Like a race? A relay team competition? An endurance event?"

Groucho sprang off the bed. Even *he* thought Kelsey's argument was silly.

"And if I'm the judge," Kelsey called after him as he pawed the door to get out of her room, "would that mean I have to kiss *all* the boys?"

The thought of kissing David Bonicelli was like flying to the top of the seesaw on the playground. The thought of kissing Adam Alldredge was like coming down hard against the ground.

Kelsey got out of bed to open the door for Groucho. "And how would I pick the *girl* winner?" she called after him as he strutted down the hallway. "Am I supposed to kiss the girls, too?"

"What in the world are you talking about?" came her mom's voice from another room.

Embarrassed at being overheard, Kelsey shut the bedroom door and fell backwards onto her bed.

"I haven't solved my problems at all," she said to the light fixture. "When the fifth grade finds out no one is getting kissed today, I'm going to be as popular as a pickle on a rope in the middle of Oklahoma."

14

Kelsey maneuvered the green bag containing her Halloween costume down the center aisle of the bus.

"Hi, Kelsey" came from every seat she passed. Smiling eyes followed her every move.

Determined to make Andrea forgive her wishy-washiness this week, Kelsey took the empty seat next to her, pulling the huge bag onto her lap.

Andrea was dressed normal today in blue jeans and a red University of Oklahoma sweatshirt. And her hair was not quite as wild as it had been all week.

She ignored Kelsey. Earphones plugged each ear. Her foot tapped, her fingers snapped, and her head bobbed to the silent music.

Kelsey left her alone, letting her get into her role as a rock star for this afternoon's Halloween party. When they arrived at school, Kelsey stumbled off the bus, hoping she hadn't bent the frame of her costume.

"Can I help you carry that?"

It was David Bonicelli.

"Sure," Kelsey replied, handing him the bag while fumbling with her books.

"What's in here?" David asked, slinging the bag over one shoulder like Santa Claus.

She looked him in the eye. What was she supposed to say? *I just gave you a giant kiss?* "It's my Halloween costume for the party this afternoon," she answered instead.

"What are you going to be?"

"It's a surprise," she said. "What are *you* going to be?"

"It's a surprise," he replied, mimicking her.

Kelsey laughed with him. She and David Bonicelli had just had a real conversation.

Mr. Hale's morning rituals were rushed today. Kelsey figured he was hurrying so the fifth-graders wouldn't miss any of his wonderful teaching because of the party.

At least it was a break from the daily boring sameness. Plus, today Mr. Hale's hair was tinted orange, probably to go with whatever costume he planned to wear that afternoon.

It was a nice change.

Change was in the air all right, Kelsey noticed, as Mr. Hale sped through their Friday spelling test. If one more person grinned and waved at her, she was going to throw up. The only person whose grin and wave mattered to her was Andrea's, and Andrea was far too quiet this morning.

Kelsey tried to catch her friend's eye during the spelling test, but Andrea's head remained bent over her paper. *No matter what it takes*, Kelsey vowed, *I'm going to smother Andrea Giese with kindness until I win back her friendship.*

Andrea had been right about Brina, Mellisa, and Molly. All they did was comb their hair and talk about boys. They didn't care about Kelsey. They didn't even *know* her. Every question they asked had something to do with the stupid contest.

They didn't know Kelsey had a cat named Groucho, or that the bedspread in her room matched the wallpaper and curtains, or that she stashed pretzels under her bed to snack on in the middle of the night, and her favorite possession in the whole world was a book about a horse, given to her by the author when Kelsey was in the third grade.

But Andrea knew all these things about her.

Andrea was her best best friend.

Kelsey opened her reading book. Somehow, it didn't surprise her that today's October holiday was *All Hallow's Eve.*

In the ninth century, people believed that the spirits of all those who'd died that year gathered at the harvest festival. If the townspeople went out that night, they wore masks and costumes to disguise themselves in case they ran into any spirits on their way to the festival.

So Kelsey had superstitious people from the ninth century to thank for getting her into the predicament she was in — right here in the twentieth century.

When Mr. Hale got out his contact lens case, Kelsey closed her reading book and got ready for the lunch bell.

She thought she'd like being popular. She thought it would mean having lots of friends. But popularity had been a lonely experience. She'd opt for one loyal friend as opposed to ten Brinas, Mellisas, and Mollys.

Maybe she should stop dreading this afternoon's Halloween party.

Maybe she should look forward to getting the kissing contest over with and being cast right back into utter obscurity for the rest of her life.

All of a sudden her former boring life didn't sound so dull after all. As a matter of fact, it sounded like a welcome change.

15

Kelsey stepped through the leg holes in the cardboard bottom of her costume, then pulled the silver frame to her neck. Sticking her arms out the openings on each side, she hooked the wire hanger shut, then smoothed the ribbon streamer the length of her costume.

She laughed at herself in the mirror, not missing the o-h-h-hs and a-h-h-hs coming from the other girls changing in the restroom. Were they just being nice, or were they really impressed with her costume?

It didn't matter, Kelsey told herself. She was impressed with her own idea for a costume.

And she was impressed with the contest she'd invented.

Sighing, she studied her teardrop shape in the mirror. Sometimes it's easier to impress yourself than to impress others.

Kelsey hurried down the hallway, tipping the cardboard so she could fit through the door of the classroom. Bits of loud conversation greeted her as kids from both fifth grades visited each desk, eating Halloween treats and showing off their costumes.

A group bobbed for apples in one corner, assisted by the other fifth-grade teacher, Mrs. Owens, who'd come to help Mr. Hale with the party.

Mr. Hale's orange hair turned out to be part of a clown costume. Now that Kelsey thought about it, Mr. Hale had been a clown last year. And the year before. And the year before.

Somehow it didn't surprise her.

Kelsey felt nervous, as if she were the afternoon's entertainment and was about to be called upon to perform.

Making her way to her desk, she dodged Adam Alldredge, who was flying around the room in his space-creature costume, burping the theme song from *Star Trek*.

The problem with making her way to her desk was that once she got there, she couldn't sit down. Instead, she gathered her notecards with the kissing trivia questions, and moved to an empty corner to study them. As she flipped through the cards, her hands trembled from dread and anticipation.

Would kids laugh at her when she explained the contest?

Would they pelt her with candy corn?

Would they boo her out of the room?

Watching Brina whisper into Mr. Hale's foot-long rubber ear, Kelsey had a feeling she was about to find out.

Suddenly she had to go to the restroom. Was it nerves, or was it the twelve trips to the water fountain this morning, trying to get Andrea's attention?

Where was Andrea anyway? Kelsey scanned the room. Had she gone home? Or was she still changing into her costume?

As Kelsey headed toward the door, Molly rushed to grab her arm. "Where are you going?" she demanded. Her eyes grew as round as the wire-framed glasses she wore, which were part of her sixties flower child costume.

"Do I need your permission to go to the bathroom?" Kelsey answered, hearing the snippiness in her own voice.

"Well, hurry." Molly twisted her zillion strands of love beads into a long coil. "We have to leave plenty of time for — " She glanced around, then winked three times. "You-know-what."

Kelsey trudged down the hallway. How was she supposed to hurry when she had to take off her entire costume to go to the bathroom, then put it back on again?

In the restroom, the wheelchair stall was the only one she could fit into. After struggling to get out of her costume, Kelsey heard a familiar voice.

Peeking through the opening between the door and the stall, she saw Andrea in full rock-and-roll attire — leather skirt, tights, and layered T-shirts. She wore every necklace, bracelet, and ring she owned, and her entire head of purple-streaked hair was spiked outward.

She'd have to use the wheelchair stall, too. It was the only one her hair would fit into.

Andrea was poised in front of the mirror, reading from a notecard. "Kelsey Minor," she was saying, "has played a big joke on the fifth grade."

Kelsey gasped. Was Andrea practicing a speech? A speech she planned to give to the entire class?

She held her breath to listen while Andrea continued. "She's made everybody believe she's going to put on a kissing contest this afternoon, but the truth is — "

Andrea looked up from her notes and stared at herself in the mirror. "The truth is," she repeated, "Kelsey Minor is a *liar*!"

Andrea pivoted on one foot, as if she'd just finished singing a song before a concert audience. "Thank you, thank you," she gushed into a pretend microphone.

Kelsey struggled to get back into her costume. Andrea was planning to expose her as a fake at the party!

She didn't need Andrea's help to expose her as a fake. She was going to expose *herself* the minute she announced the trivia contest.

Shoving her arms through the cutout holes, Kelsey knew she had to face Andrea and have it out with her right now, right here in the girls' restroom.

But by the time Kelsey had wriggled back into her costume, Andrea had gone back to class. How could she get her friend alone now?

Kelsey walked as slowly as she could down the hallway, one foot in front of the other. She imagined she was Wendy from *Peter Pan*, on Captain Hook's pirate ship, walking the plank. Three more steps to the end. Beyond that, the churning ocean —

"Come on, come on, come on." Molly's whining voice snapped her out of the daydream. The flower child, wearing a peasant dress and sandals, leaned into the hallway and motioned for Kelsey to hurry up.

Kelsey stepped past her into the classroom, resisting the urge to stuff a handful of Molly's love beads into her mouth to shut her up.

"There she is!" Mr. Hale exclaimed. The teacher blew on his clown whistle to get everyone's attention, then motioned to Brina. Laughter and voices in the room hushed instantly, as if Mr. Hale's whistle had suddenly clicked off Kelsey's hearing.

Brina stepped to the front of the room. She was dressed as a princess and was wearing a real rhinestone crown that Kelsey would die for. "It's time," Brina began.

Kelsey wondered why Brina felt it was her job to announce the contest at all. What did *she* have to do with it?

"We've all been eagerly waiting for this afternoon, so we can hold our class's first kissing contest."

As the class applauded, Kelsey was sure she heard Mr. Hale and Mrs. Owens gasp.

Brina curtseyed like a real princess. "Now, I'd like to introduce Kelsey Minor, who will explain the kissing contest." She gave a royal flip of her arm in Kelsey's direction, swirling the lace robe she wore.

Kelsey hated the way Brina acted as if she knew all about the kissing contest when she didn't. And she hated the way Molly was jumping up and down behind Brina huffing and puffing, "Come on, come on, come on."

But even more than that, she hated the way Andrea was making her way to the front of the room, holding the notecards with their *Kelsey-is-a-liar* speech.

16

Grumbles skittered through the room as Andrea took her place in the spotlight instead of Kelsey.

Kelsey's heart skittered along with the grumbles. Was Andrea really planning to give a hate speech about her own best friend?

She thinks there's no contest, Kelsey, because the last time you talked to her, there was no contest.

Right, she told herself. But now there is.

Only Andrea doesn't know that, because you've stopped being her best friend.

But —

You have, Kelsey, you've stopped being Andrea's best friend. And now, your ex-best friend is about to get even.

Andrea cleared her throat and jingled her jewelry. "All of you are expecting Kelsey Minor to put on a kissing contest right now, aren't you?"

"Yeahs" came from around the room.

"Give the stage to Kelsey," someone hollered. A few kids began to boo Andrea under their breath, calling her *Aug*.

"Well," Andrea continued in a shaky voice, "I want to tell you the truth. The truth about the kissing contest and the truth about Kelsey Minor."

The booing got louder.

Mr. Hale looked confused, as if he'd never encountered this sort of thing in his *How to Be a Teacher* manual.

Kelsey felt as if she were in an oven.

Like a baked potato wrapped in aluminum foil.

No matter what terrible things Andrea was getting ready to say about her, there was no way Kelsey could stand here and let the class boo her former best friend.

"Kel-sey, Kel-sey, Kel-sey," the class began to chant.

Andrea looked as if she were about to cry.

Kelsey hurried to the front of the room, bumping kids out of the way with her wide cardboard hips.

The chanting stopped.

"Thank you, Andrea," she said, then faced the class. "Andrea was *trying* to introduce the kissing contest." Her voice wavered over the word *contest*. Kelsey glared at the class. "Andrea was *helping* me. She's my best friend."

As if on cue, everyone looked at the floor. Kelsey felt a great sense of power at shaming the fifth grade.

Andrea was staring at her as if she'd never seen a giant Hershey's Kiss before. Of course, she probably hadn't, but that was beside the point.

Kelsey crossed her arms the way Mr. Hale did when he was displeased with his students. "I'm not sure I want to begin my kissing contest at all if you're going to be mean to my best friend."

A few "I'm sorry, Andreas" came from around the room.

Kelsey waited.

More "I'm sorrys" filled the air.

Within moments, everyone was apologizing to Andrea, who was standing so still, none of her jewelry even jingled.

Out of the corner of her eye, Kelsey saw Mr. Hale glance at his watch. She'd better hurry or there'd be no time left for the contest.

Yesterday that would have suited her just fine. But today, she was ready. For better or worse, it was time.

She was on.

This was it.

"Let's begin."

Molly rushed to the front, thrusting a whistle at Kelsey. She cupped her hands around her mouth, whispering, "Remember the first rule."

"Right," Kelsey said as Molly rushed back to her seat.

Andrea began to edge toward her desk. Kelsey caught her arm. "No, you have to help me."

Andrea grinned at her.

"We're in this together, remember?" Kelsey whispered.

Andrea's grin widened until her eyes twinkled. "So, do it," she whispered back.

As Kelsey divided the class into two teams, the room instantly came alive. Kids began to squirm, shuffle papers, cough.

Molly was a further distraction, dashing back and forth to the drinking fountain, filling everyone's punch cup with water.

Rule number six, Kelsey reminded herself.

All across the room, hands shot up:

"Mr. Hale, I'm not feeling well. Can I go to the nurse?"

"Mr. Hale, my mom is coming to get me early today, and she asked me to wait outside."

"Mr. Hale, I promised Ms. McFarland I'd help her inventory soccer equipment this afternoon."

Kelsey peered at the kids causing the interruptions. What was going on?

The fifth-graders had practically been counting the minutes until the kissing contest began, and now they were trying to get out of it?

Why?

Feet shuffled, pencils flipped to the floor, arguments began. Those who'd asked to leave, gathered their things and stood up.

The answer came to Kelsey like a surprise chorus of "Trick or treat!"

Kids were nervous. They were scared. They thought they'd soon be kissing somebody.

And they really didn't want to.

Not now.

Not here.

Not in front of everyone.

Kelsey studied faces around the room. All of them looked as scared as if they'd seen a real Halloween ghost. Even Mellisa, Brina, and Molly.

So, it was true.

Kelsey almost burst out laughing.

The entire fifth grade was absolutely terrified of her little kissing contest.

17

The sense of power Kelsey felt earlier surged through her veins, like sweet Halloween candy in her blood. "Sit down," she ordered.

Kids sat.

"Quit fidgeting."

Fidgeting stopped.

"The kissing contest has begun. No one can leave the room."

Kelsey heard Andrea giggling and jingling behind her. She felt glad her friend had returned to normal.

Normal for Andrea, that is.

"Here's how the contest works. I will ask team number one a trivia question about kissing. If the player has the correct answer, his or her team gets a point."

Kelsey had never heard her voice sound so strong and clear in front of the class before. "If the player gives the wrong answer, team number two gets one chance to answer. Andrea will keep score on the board. And the winning team gets a special surprise.

"Are you ready?"

Sixty pairs of eyes watched her while heads bobbed up and down.

Kelsey liked being in charge. She felt as if she could tell the class to do anything — like two hundred long-division problems — and they would get out their math books without question.

But she'd never do that, she told herself, glancing at Mr. Hale. He was blotting his forehead with a green polka-dotted clown handkerchief, which matched his green polka-dotted clown tie.

"Question number one."

Kelsey moved to the first player on team one. As she opened her mouth to ask the trivia question of the gray walrus, who was nibbling cookies between his tusks, she noticed for the first time who the walrus was.

David Bonicelli.

Kelsey's sense of power dissolved, as if she were made of real chocolate inside her Hershey's Kiss costume.

David stared at her.

She stared at David.

Mr. Hale stared at his watch.

Molly's voice inside Kelsey's head said, *Come on, come on, come on.* It made her feel strong again.

"Question number one," she repeated, holding David's gaze. *"How do Eskimos kiss?"*

The room was so quiet, not one candy wrapper rattled.

David rose in his seat, leaning forward. His plastic tusks banged against his desktop as he motioned for her to come closer.

What was he doing? Kelsey leaned as close to him as she dared.

David cleared his throat, then whispered. "Do you want me to *show* you how Eskimos kiss, or *tell* you?"

Kelsey's chocolate heart melted at the thought of rubbing noses with David Bonicelli.

She started to laugh, then swallowed the urge, for fear he'd think she was laughing at him. *"Tell* me," she whispered back, feeling disappointed by her answer.

David grinned, looking like one relieved walrus as he relaxed in his chair, cocking his head to one side. "Are you going to blow the whistle so I can begin?"

Kelsey swallowed another laugh, blowing a short blast on Molly's whistle.

Drawing himself up straight, David proclaimed loud and clear, "Eskimos kiss by rubbing noses."

His team cheered at his correct answer, while Andrea recorded the point on the chalkboard. Mr.

Hale and Mrs. Owens exchanged relieved glances, then joined in the cheering.

The contest was on.

Kelsey moved from team to team, asking questions and blowing the whistle:

"What does S.W.A.K. mean?

"Why did noblemen kiss a lady's hand in the time of chivalry?

"Where are Hershey's Kisses made?

"Name a rock group that became famous for wearing bizarre makeup.

"What are sometimes called 'kisses from angels'?"

The contest went fast, as Kelsey shot questions to one team member after another.

Players hollered encouragement to each other, saying things like "Don't hold your breath," and "Give it all you've got."

Andrea even helped by making up more questions, jotting them on scraps of paper, then handing them to Kelsey as she moved between the teams.

The clock determined the end of the kissing contest. The lead had switched back and forth from team one to team two so many times, Kelsey called the score a tie and rewarded both teams with Hershey's Kisses.

"Way to go Kelsey!" Mellisa hollered when the contest ended, starting off a round of applause.

It startled Kelsey. She absorbed the approval coming from Mellisa, Brina, and Molly. They weren't mad at her after all.

She glanced at all the kids as she handed out prizes. No one was angry at her.

And the reason was because she'd let them off the hook.

She hadn't made them kiss anybody. Fifth-graders would rather *talk* about kissing while eating chocolate kisses, than —

Well, *David Bonicelli* had wanted to. Kelsey blushed at the thought. Maybe not *kiss*, but *rub noses*. If they lived in Alaska, that might mean they were boyfriend and girlfriend.

"Thank you, Kelsey," said Mr. Hale. One of his rubber ears was lopsided. "That was terrific. Can you stay a minute and help clean up?" Kelsey nodded as class was dismissed.

"I'll save you a seat on the bus," Andrea said, collecting her own bag of kisses. "And Kel." Andrea straightened Kelsey's white streamer. "Thanks for still being my friend."

Kelsey gave her an extra bag of kisses. She knew she'd sit with Andrea every day from now on — at lunch, on the bus, or on the playground.

It was okay to have lots of friends, but it was special to have one best friend.

Before Kelsey helped clean up, she rushed into the restroom to change into regular clothes for the bus trip home. When she returned, the classroom was empty.

Except for Adam Alldredge. He whizzed by on his way out the door, giving her a chocolate grin as he burped *good-bye*.

Kelsey cleaned up quickly so she wouldn't miss the bus.

"That was a neat contest," came a voice from behind her.

It was the walrus. He'd removed his tusks so he could talk better.

"Thanks."

Kelsey felt shy all of a sudden. If the kissing contest accomplished anything at all this week, it had made David Bonicelli know she was alive.

Kelsey hefted the leftover paper plates, reaching high to return them to the top shelf of the storage cabinet.

"Let me help," said David, putting his hands under hers and guiding the plates into place.

As Kelsey lowered her arms, David leaned over and kissed her on the cheek. "Have a fun Halloween," he whispered, then raced on flippered feet through the outside door before she could answer.

Kelsey placed one palm over David's kiss, wanting to seal it into her cheek forever.

Suddenly it hit her.

The Friday afternoon she'd dreaded all week had come and gone. And she'd done what she set out to do.

The kissing contest had been a success.

Not only a success, but there'd even been a grand-prize winner:

Kelsey Minor.

The only fifth-grader who'd actually gotten kissed.

She was the winner of her own kissing contest.

♥

ANSWERS TO THE KISSING TRIVIA
QUESTIONS ASKED
DURING THE CONTEST:

What does S.W.A.K. mean?
Sealed with a kiss

Why did noblemen kiss a lady's hand in the time
of chivalry?
To greet them with respect

Where are Hershey's Kisses made?
In Hershey, Pennsylvania

Name the rock group that became famous for
wearing bizarre makeup.
KISS

What are sometimes called "kisses from angels"?
Freckles

ANSWERS TO QUESTIONS FROM CHAPTER 12:

How did the custom of kissing begin?
As a human instinct

Why does the groom kiss the bride at the end of the wedding ceremony?
To seal their wedding vows

Why do movie stars pretend to kiss in greeting, but don't?
So they won't mess up their lipstick

About the Author

DIAN CURTIS REGAN has never competed in a Kissing Contest, although she plans to keep practicing in case the opportunity should arise. She eats a lot of spaghetti and always observes Potato Days. And, she is the author of eight books for young readers, which she writes from her home office in Oklahoma.

APPLE PAPERBACKS

Pick an Apple and Polish Off Some Great Reading!

NEW APPLE TITLES

☐	MT43356-3	Family Picture Dean Hughes	$2.75
☐	MT41682-0	Dear Dad, Love Laurie Susan Beth Pfeffer	$2.75
☐	MT41529-8	My Sister, the Creep	
		Candice F. Ransom	$2.75

BESTSELLING APPLE TITLES

☐	MT42709-1	Christina's Ghost Betty Ren Wright	$2.75
☐	MT43461-6	The Dollhouse Murders Betty Ren Wright	$2.75
☐	MT42319-3	The Friendship Pact Susan Beth Pfeffer	$2.75
☐	MT43444-6	Ghosts Beneath Our Feet Betty Ren Wright	$2.75
☐	MT40605-1	Help! I'm a Prisoner in the Library Eth Clifford	$2.50
☐	MT42193-X	Leah's Song Eth Clifford	$2.50
☐	MT43618-X	Me and Katie (The Pest) Ann M. Martin	$2.75
☐	MT42883-7	Sixth Grade Can Really Kill You Barthe DeClements	$2.75
☐	MT40409-1	Sixth Grade Secrets Louis Sachar	$2.75
☐	MT42882-9	Sixth Grade Sleepover Eve Bunting	$2.75
☐	MT41732-0	Too Many Murphys	
		Colleen O'Shaughnessy McKenna	$2.75
☐	MT41118-7	Tough-Luck Karen Johanna Hurwitz	$2.50
☐	MT42326-6	Veronica the Show-off Nancy K. Robinson	$2.75

Available wherever you buy books...or use the coupon below.

Scholastic Inc., P.O. Box 7502, 2932 East McCarty Street, Jefferson City, MO 65102

Please send me the books I have checked above. I am enclosing $_____ (please add $2.00 to cover shipping and handling). Send check or money order — no cash or C.O.D. s please.

Name _____

Address _____

City _____ State/Zip _____

Please allow four to six weeks for delivery. Offer good in the U.S.A. only.
Sorry, mail orders are not available to residents of Canada. Prices subject to change.

APP1089

America's Favorite Series

THE BABY-SITTERS CLUB

by Ann M. Martin

Collect Them All!

The seven girls at Stoneybrook Middle School get into all kinds of adventures...with school, boys, and, of course, baby-sitting!

☐ MG41588-3	Baby-sitters on Board! Super Special #1	$2.95
☐ MG41583-2	#19 Claudia and the Bad Joke	$2.75
☐ MG42004-6	#20 Kristy and the Walking Disaster	$2.75
☐ MG42005-4	#21 Mallory and the Trouble with Twins	$2.75
☐ MG42006-2	#22 Jessi Ramsey, Pet-sitter	$2.75
☐ MG42007-0	#23 Dawn on the Coast	$2.75
☐ MG42002-X	#24 Kristy and the Mother's Day Surprise	$2.75
☐ MG42003-8	#25 Mary Anne and the Search for Tigger	$2.75
☐ MG42419-X	Baby-sitters' Summer Vacation Super Special #2	$2.95
☐ MG42503-X	#26 Claudia and the Sad Good-bye	$2.95
☐ MG42502-1	#27 Jessi and the Superbrat	$2.95
☐ MG42501-3	#28 Welcome Back, Stacey!	$2.95
☐ MG42500-5	#29 Mallory and the Mystery Diary	$2.95
☐ MG42499-8	Baby-sitters' Winter Vacation Super Special #3	$2.95
☐ MG42498-X	#30 Mary Anne and the Great Romance	$2.95
☐ MG42497-1	#31 Dawn's Wicked Stepsister	$2.95
☐ MG42496-3	#32 Kristy and the Secret of Susan	$2.95
☐ MG42495-5	#33 Claudia and the Mystery of Stoneybrook	$2.95
☐ MG42494-7	#34 Mary Anne and Too Many Boys	$2.95
☐ MG42508-0	#35 Stacey and the New Kids on the Block	$2.95

For a complete listing of all the Baby-sitter Club titles write to :
Customer Service at the address below.

Available wherever you buy books...or use the coupon below.

SLEEPOVER FRIENDS™

by Susan Saunders

☐ MF40641-8 **#1 Patti's Luck**	$2.50	
☐ MF40642-6 **#2 Staring Stephanie!**	$2.50	
☐ MF40643-4 **#3 Kate's Surprise**	$2.50	
☐ MF40644-2 **#4 Patti's New Look**	$2.50	
☐ MF41336-8 **#5 Lauren's Big Mix-Up**	$2.50	
☐ MF42662-1 **Sleepover Friends' Super Sleepover Guide**	$2.50	
☐ MF42366-5 **#16 Kate's Crush**	$2.50	
☐ MF42367-3 **#17 Patti Gets Even**	$2.50	
☐ MF42814-4 **#18 Stephanie and the Magician**	$2.50	
☐ MF42815-2 **#19 The Great Kate**	$2.50	
☐ MF42816-0 **#20 Lauren in the Middle**	$2.50	
☐ MF42817-9 **#21 Starstruck Stephanie**	$2.50	
☐ MF42818-7 **#22 The Trouble with Patti**	$2.50	

☐ MF42819-5 **#23 Kate's Surprise Visitor**	$2.50	
☐ MF43194-3 **#24 Lauren's New Friend**	$2.50	
☐ MF43193-5 **#25 Stephanie and the Wedding**	$2.50	
☐ MF43192-7 **#26 The New Kate**	$2.50	
☐ MF43190-0 **#27 Where's Patti?**	$2.50	
☐ MF43191-9 **#28 Lauren's New Address**	$2.50	
☐ MF43189-7 **#29 Kate the Boss**	$2.50	
☐ MF43929-4 **#30 Big Sister Stephanie**	$2.75	
☐ MF43928-6 **#31 Lauren's After-school Job**	$2.75	
☐ MF43927-8 **#32 A Valentine for Patti** (Jan. '91)	$2.75	
☐ MF43926-X **#33 Lauren's Double Disaster** (Feb. '91)	$2.75	

Available wherever you buy books...or use this order form.

Scholastic Inc. P.O. Box 7502, 2931 E. McCarty Street, Jefferson City, MO 65102

Please send me the books I have checked above. I am enclosing $_____
(please add $2.00 to cover shipping and handling). Send check or money order—no cash or C.O.D.s please.

Name _____

Address _____

City_____ State/Zip _____

Please allow four to six weeks for delivery. Offer good in U.S.A. only. Sorry, mail orders are not available to residents of Canada. Prices subject to change.

SLE690